Heroes and Villains of Ancient Rome

Adam Ford

Contents

Portraits in Ancient Rome

> *"What we wish,*
> *we readily believe ..."*
>
> **Julius Caesar,**
> ***Commentarii de Bello Gallico***

History often paints colourful pictures of the leaders of ancient Rome as either heroes or villains. But are these pictures realistic portraits? Or were these people more complex than we are led to believe? When reading about the past, it is important to understand that many historical accounts are a mix of fact and fiction.

In this book, we look at four famous figures from the time of ancient Rome: Julius Caesar, Queen Cleopatra of Egypt, Augustus Caesar and Nero, and explore whether history shows them as they really were.

Julius Caesar
(100–44 BCE)

Queen Cleopatra of Egypt
(69–30 BCE)

If we examine historical accounts written at or around the time when these people were alive, we can sometimes get a clearer and more accurate image of the past. These **contemporary** histories are called primary historical sources of information.

Primary historical sources can be written accounts, poems, art or even visual depictions on coins. Ancient Roman historians, such as Suetonius, Tacitus and Plutarch, wrote about the important people and leaders who shaped their world.

However, often these primary histories are not simply factual accounts describing who these people were or what they did.

These portraits are an artist's impression of what these ancient leaders looked like, based on statues of them.

Augustus Caesar
(63 BCE–14 **CE**)

Nero
(37–68 CE)

Sometimes, accounts by ancient historians were created to make particular leaders look good, perhaps because the historians were scared they would be punished if they didn't write them that way! There are also historical accounts that deliberately focus on and exaggerate the bad deeds and nature of a person. Often, these accounts were written after the person had died. Deliberate, or intentional, **distortions** of the truth are called conscious historical bias.

Historical bias can also be unintentional. For instance, Suetonius and other ancient Roman historians wrote from positions of **privilege**. These historians were male, were free citizens, and were very wealthy. The lives of most women, **enslaved** people and the poorer, common people are absent from their writings. They didn't think of these people as important. These inaccuracies are called unconscious historical bias.

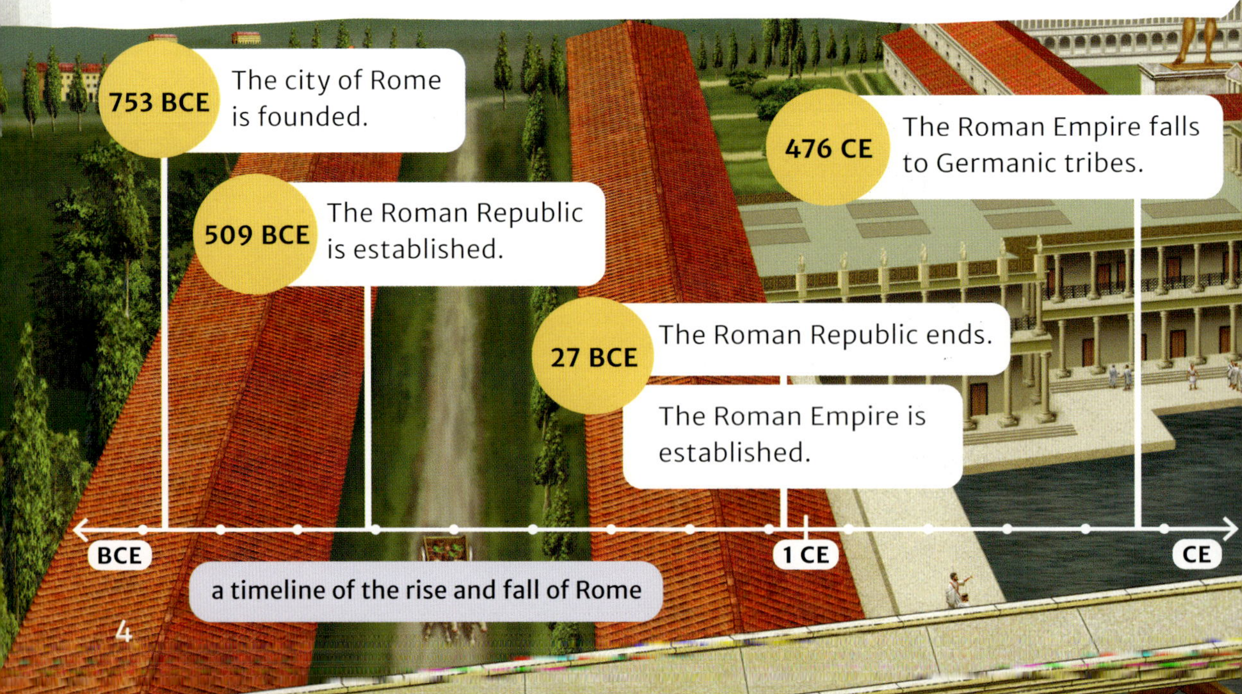

a timeline of the rise and fall of Rome

Julius Caesar and Augustus Caesar greatly expanded the Roman Empire to include places like Britannia (England), Gaul (now France) and Aegyptus (Egypt).

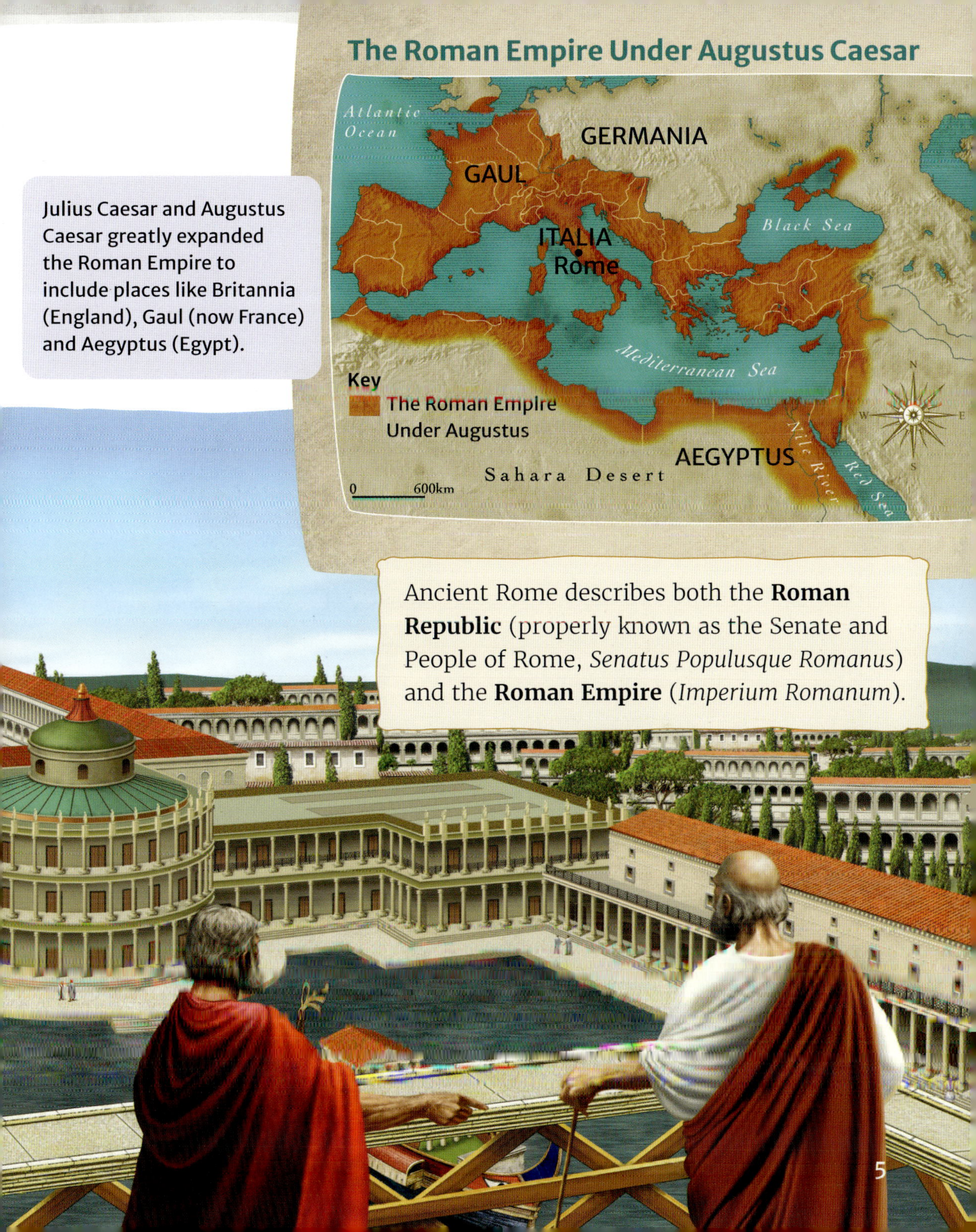

Ancient Rome describes both the **Roman Republic** (properly known as the Senate and People of Rome, *Senatus Populusque Romanus*) and the **Roman Empire** (*Imperium Romanum*).

Julius Caesar

(12 July 100 BCE – 15 March 44 BCE)

"Veni, vidi, vici."
(I came, I saw, I conquered.)

Julius Caesar, from Suetonius

Gaius Julius Caesar was a Roman general and politician who governed the Roman Republic from 48 BCE until his death by **assassination** in 44 BCE. He was both admired and feared as a powerful leader and military genius.

Julius Caesar created the first version of the modern Western calendar, gave his name to the month of July and passed on his title of "Caesar" to every Roman emperor that followed.

This is one of many ancient marble busts of Julius Caesar.

Before governing the Roman Republic in 48 BCE, Julius Caesar led his army on a **campaign** in Gaul (the ancient name for western Europe) for eight years (58–50 BCE). He defeated many of the **Gallic** tribes, stealing their lands. Caesar even wrote a rather heroic and glowing description of himself and his military conquests in his book *Commentarii de Bello Gallico* (*Commentaries on the Gallic War*), which you can still read today!

Julius Caesar leads his army in Gaul.

The Death of Caesar (*La morte di Cesare*) in the Roman senate was portrayed by painter Vincenzo Camuccini in 1805.

Caesar's military success made him popular with both his army and the Roman people. This popularity made him powerful and a threat to the current political leaders of the Roman Republic. Caesar was therefore declared a traitor by his once great friend, the politician Pompey Magnus.

Angered by his friend's betrayal, Caesar and his loyal army marched on the city of Rome in 49 BCE and finally defeated Pompey during a bloody **civil war**. Caesar then made himself "dictator for life" (*dictator perpetuus*) in 44 BCE, a title and role that provides insight into his not-so-modest ambitions.

Those who were against Caesar were thrown out of Rome, bullied into supporting him or put to death.

Caesar's grip on power threatened the democratic foundations of the Roman Republic, which relied on rule being shared by more than one person and power being kept in check by the **senate**. Only four years into his dictatorship, a group of senators (Roman politicians) killed Julius Caesar in the senate house on 15 March 44 BCE.

Caesar's conquest of Gaul resulted in the enslavement or death of hundreds of thousands of people. His march on Rome made him a traitor to the Republic and caused a civil war. Both his friends and his enemies were sacrificed for his ruthless ambition. None of this makes Caesar particularly heroic, yet he is regarded as a great Roman and as one of the most influential historical figures ever. Why is that?

Caesar was excellent at promoting himself, not only through writing his own versions of his deeds, but also by reproducing images of himself in paintings, statues and, for the first time, on Roman coinage. In many instances, his own words are the only primary sources we have for his life.

This bronze statue of Julius Caesar still stands in the city of Rome.

This silver Roman coin from 44 BCE depicts Julius Caesar.

Over the years, Caesar's words have been repeated, but rarely challenged, by historians, and made popular by the famous writer of plays William Shakespeare, until Caesar's biased accounts were considered fact. There are even Hollywood movies about Caesar.

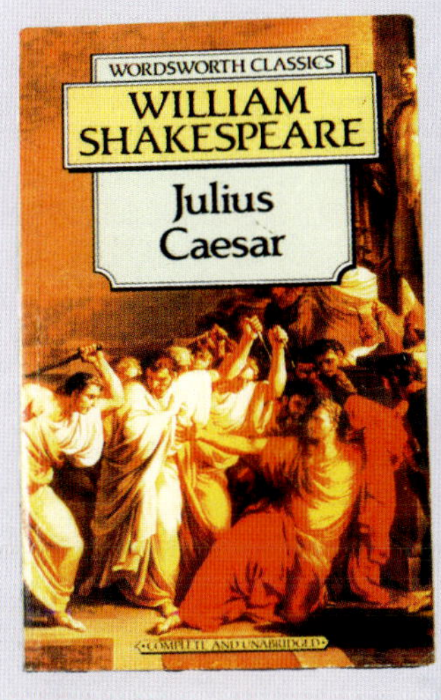

That is how history works, in some ways. Caesar may have even acknowledged it himself with this reported quote: "In the end, it is impossible not to become what others believe you are."

The 1953 movie *Julius Caesar* is one of many films made about Caesar.

Queen Cleopatra of Egypt

(69 BCE – 12 August 30 BCE)

> *"I will not be triumphed over!"*
>
> **Cleopatra, from Livy**

Cleopatra VII Thea Philopator, better known as Queen Cleopatra of Egypt, was the last queen of the vast Ptolemaic (pronounced *tol-oh-may-ic*) **dynasty** of Egypt, ruling from 51 to 30 BCE. She was a scholar, a clever political operator and an influential partner of two of the most powerful men in ancient Rome: Julius Caesar and Mark Antony (Marcus Antonius). Yet, Cleopatra is mostly remembered for ending her life with the help of a snake.

The Ptolemaic Kingdom Under Cleopatra VII

The Ptolemaic dynasty of Egypt began with the ruler Ptolemy I in 323 BCE. The nearby Parthian Empire and Nabatean Kingdom are now many different countries, including Turkey and Saudi Arabia.

It is remarkable that even though Cleopatra was a very important and powerful figure in both Egypt and Rome, there are no surviving contemporary accounts of her life.

Why was so very little written about Cleopatra, when there are so many accounts of figures who lived at the same time, such as Julius Caesar?

One possible reason is because Cleopatra was a woman.

This ancient Roman marble bust of Cleopatra dates back to 40–30 BCE.

Cleopatra was also represented in Egyptian art on the outer wall of the Temple of Hathor at Dendera, Egypt.

Historical gender bias describes the imbalance of historical accounts about significant male and female figures from history. An obvious gender bias is the bias of **omission**. Women have been left out of many ancient historical accounts. If they were included, they were depicted in a way that reinforced **stereotypes** and focused on their appearance or who they were married to, rather than their achievements.

However, it is possible to piece together an incomplete picture of Cleopatra. We can compare later historical accounts of her from writers such as Plutarch and Suetonius, as well as the Greek historian Cassius Dio. The image that emerges is of an interesting and complex character.

Plutarch describes Cleopatra as being charming and of high intelligence. It is said that she spoke many languages as well as her native Greek (although born in Egypt, Cleopatra was Greek Macedonian). She was a philosopher, scientist and mathematician, who filled her royal court with people of learning.

The painting *Cleopatra on the Terraces of Philae* by Frederick Arthur Bridgman imagines what Cleopatra might have looked like.

A good relationship with Rome was necessary to Cleopatra's survival as Queen of Egypt. Her rule was under constant threat from enemies. She needed the might of Rome to help maintain her throne. On the other hand, Rome needed Egypt's wheat exports to feed its citizens.

Cleopatra's relationship with the Roman **consul** Mark Antony secured her throne, but also pulled her into a struggle for power between Mark Antony and another Roman leader, Gaius Octavius, who would later become the first Roman emperor, using the name Augustus Caesar.

The struggle between Mark Antony and Gaius Octavius turned into a civil war. Antony and Cleopatra's armies fought against the armies of Rome. In 31 BCE, Gaius Octavius defeated Mark Antony and Cleopatra in a sea battle off the coast of Greece, at Actium.

Cleopatra is depicted on this ancient Greek gold coin from 36 BCE.

This Roman silver coin shows Mark Antony.

Fleeing back to Egypt, Mark Antony and Cleopatra took their own lives in 30 BCE rather than be captured by Gaius Octavius. If captured, they would have been paraded in chains through the streets of Rome in a spectacle known as a "Triumph", before being killed.

Popular accounts say that Cleopatra ended her life by allowing a venomous snake to bite her. It is said that before the snake's venom put an end to her remarkable life, Cleopatra declared, "I will not be triumphed over!"

The Flight of Antony and Cleopatra from the Battle of Actium is shown in this 1897 painting by Agnes Pringle.

Augustus Caesar

(23 September 63 BCE – 19 August 14 CE)

Augustus Caesar is often regarded as the greatest emperor of Rome and one of the greatest leaders of the ancient world. He was born Gaius Octavius or "Octavian", but changed his name to Augustus Caesar when he became the first emperor of the Roman Empire. The month of August was renamed in his honour.

> *"I found Rome a city of bricks and left it a city of marble."*
>
> **Augustus Caesar, from Suetonius**

As the longest ruling Roman emperor, Augustus created the Roman Empire out of the ashes of the fallen Roman Republic. He oversaw a period of peace and **prosperity** never before experienced by Roman citizens. This time of peace extended over 150 years after his death, and is known as *Pax Romana* (Roman Peace).

This ancient bust of Augustus Caesar, made from marble, was one of many such statues of the first emperor of Rome.

Augustus, when he was still called Gaius Octavius, first ruled the Roman Republic along with two powerful politicians and military generals: Mark Antony and Marcus Lepidus. However, Augustus had ambitions to reinvent Rome under a single leader – himself. Augustus defeated Antony and Lepidus in a civil war and proclaimed himself "first citizen" (*princeps civitatis*), with the new name Augustus Caesar (*Augustus* meaning majestic or great in Latin, and Caesar a reference to his adoptive father, Julius Caesar).

Mark Antony (left), Gaius Octavius (middle) and Marcus Lepidus (right) met on a river island near Bologna to form their alliance.

Over the last two thousand years, contemporary and ancient historians have argued about whether Augustus Caesar was good or bad. But they all agree that he was a very hard-working leader. During his 40 years as emperor, Augustus vastly increased the size of the Roman Empire, rebuilt the city of Rome, built a huge network of roads, established a police force and fire brigade, and created Rome's first permanent army.

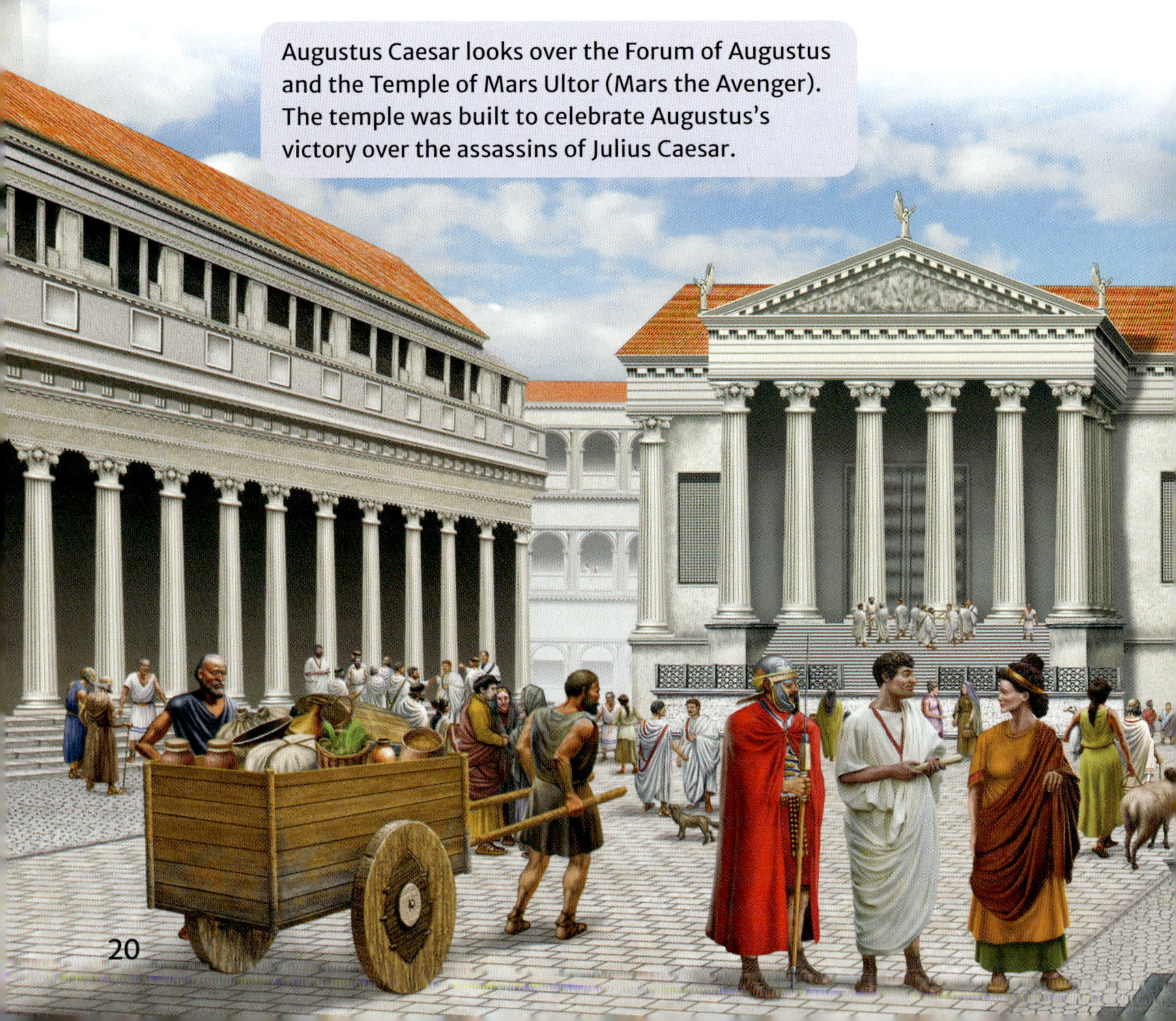

Augustus Caesar looks over the Forum of Augustus and the Temple of Mars Ultor (Mars the Avenger). The temple was built to celebrate Augustus's victory over the assassins of Julius Caesar.

Augustus Caesar's political success was the result of **bribing** senators in return for their unquestioning support. He also gave himself many powers. His position and influence were enforced by a loyal army. How Augustus ruled the Roman Empire became a model for future Roman emperors for the next 1400 years. And such was his reputation that every Roman emperor after him also took the names "Caesar Augustus".

However, Augustus was also ruthless, cruel and driven by an ambition for power that he pursued with deadly results. Anyone who stood in his way often met a grizzly end. His ambition led him to become the most powerful figure in the history of ancient Rome up to that point.

This Roman silver coin depicts Augustus Caesar.

So, who was Augustus? Was he a great leader who brought peace and prosperity to the empire, or a scheming **tyrant**?

Historical evidence suggests that Augustus was probably both. He got rid of anyone who stood in his way. But once emperor, his fierce **patriotism** and efficient and skilled ruling style brought considerable benefits to the citizens of Rome. Selfishness and selflessness existed together to create a complex and hugely important historical figure.

The Ara Pacis Augustae shrine in Rome's Field of Mars celebrates peace under Augustus Caesar.

"... the motive of Octavian, the future Augustus, was lust for power ... there had certainly been peace, but it was a bloodstained peace ..."

Tacitus, the *Annals* Book I

This marble statue of Augustus Caesar found in Prima Porta, Rome, dates back to the first century CE.

Nero

(15 December 37 CE – 9 June 68 CE)

Nero Claudius Caesar Augustus Germanicus, or Nero, was the fifth emperor of Rome. He became ruler of the Roman Empire at the age of sixteen. After fourteen years, Nero was overthrown by the senate and forced to take his own life, aged 30.

> *"Nero watched the destruction … enraptured by what he called 'the beauty of the flames …'"*
>
> **Nero, from Suetonius**

By most accounts, Nero was a dreadful person. Ancient historians such as Suetonius, Tacitus and Cassius Dio describe Nero as a cruel and corrupt tyrant. Some claim that he was responsible for the great fire of Rome (July 64 CE) which destroyed two thirds of the city, so that he could clear enough space to build himself a huge palace – the Golden House.

This marble bust depicts the Roman emperor Nero.

While his early reign was an example of calm and efficient governing, Nero cannot take the credit. There is little evidence that Nero had much involvement in the running of the Roman Empire while he was still a teenager. Instead, it is thought that his mother, Agrippina the Younger, was the real power, and ruled Rome through her son.

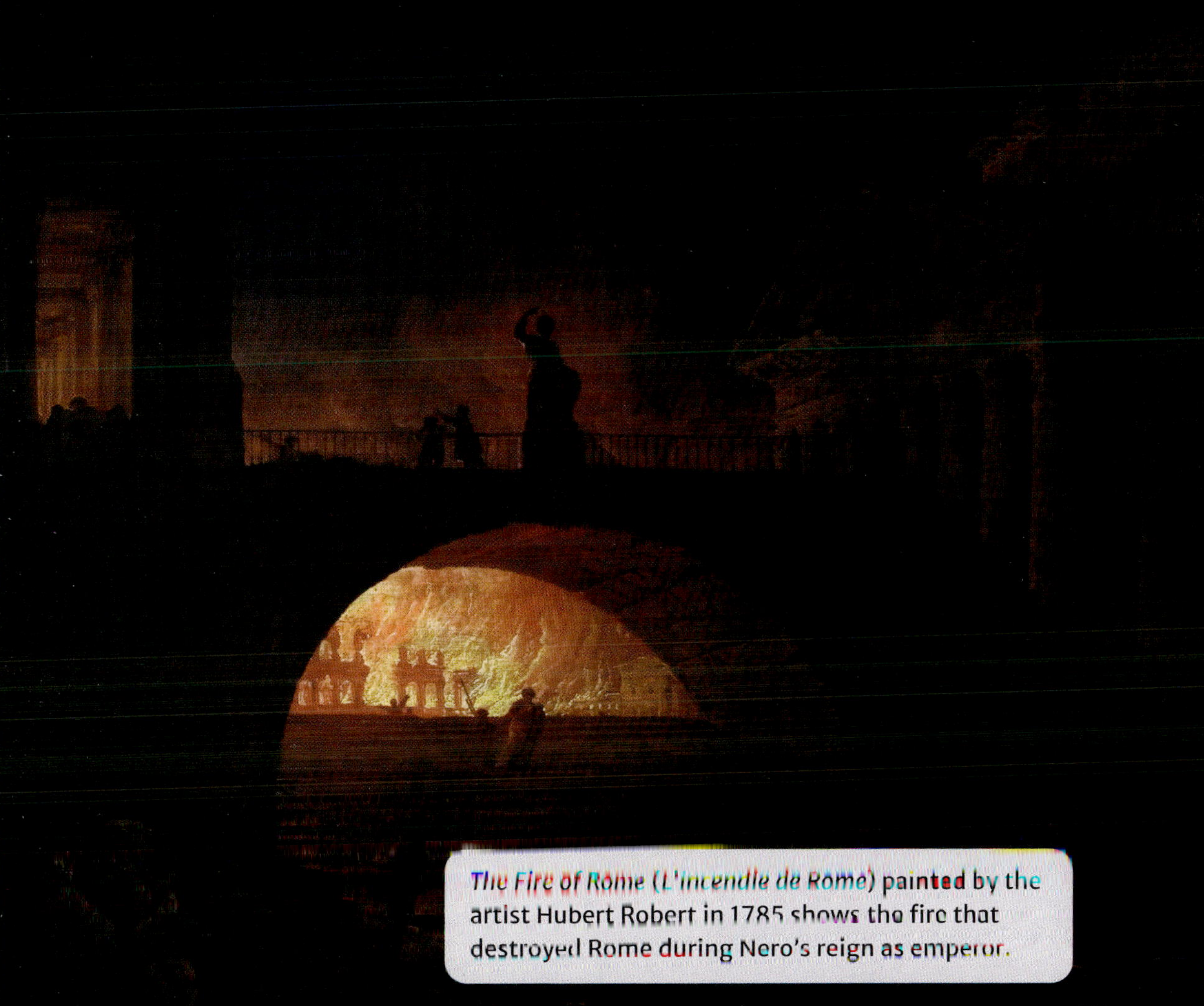

The Fire of Rome (L'incendie de Rome) painted by the artist Hubert Robert in 1785 shows the fire that destroyed Rome during Nero's reign as emperor.

As Nero became an adult, he was increasingly frustrated by Agrippina's control, and arranged for her to die in a planned shipwreck. She survived and swam to shore, only to be killed later that evening.

After Agrippina's death, Nero appeared to lose all sense of right and wrong, believing that there were constant plots against his rule. He wasted enormous amounts of money on grand public works and large homes for himself, like the Golden House, which included an artificial lake and indoor waterfall. He hosted lavish feasts that lasted from dawn until dusk, a lifestyle that was vastly different to the lives of everyday Romans.

This Roman silver coin depicts Agrippina the Younger, Nero's mother.

Eventually, Nero's behaviour became too much. Declared a public enemy by the senate, he was forced to flee Rome. On 9 June 68 CE, with the Roman army closing in, he ordered an ex-slave to end his life.

But was Nero really as terrible as historical accounts describe? It is difficult to be certain, because there are no historical documents created during his lifetime that have survived. Most of what we know of Nero comes from Suetonius and Tacitus, who wrote their accounts 50 years after Nero's death.

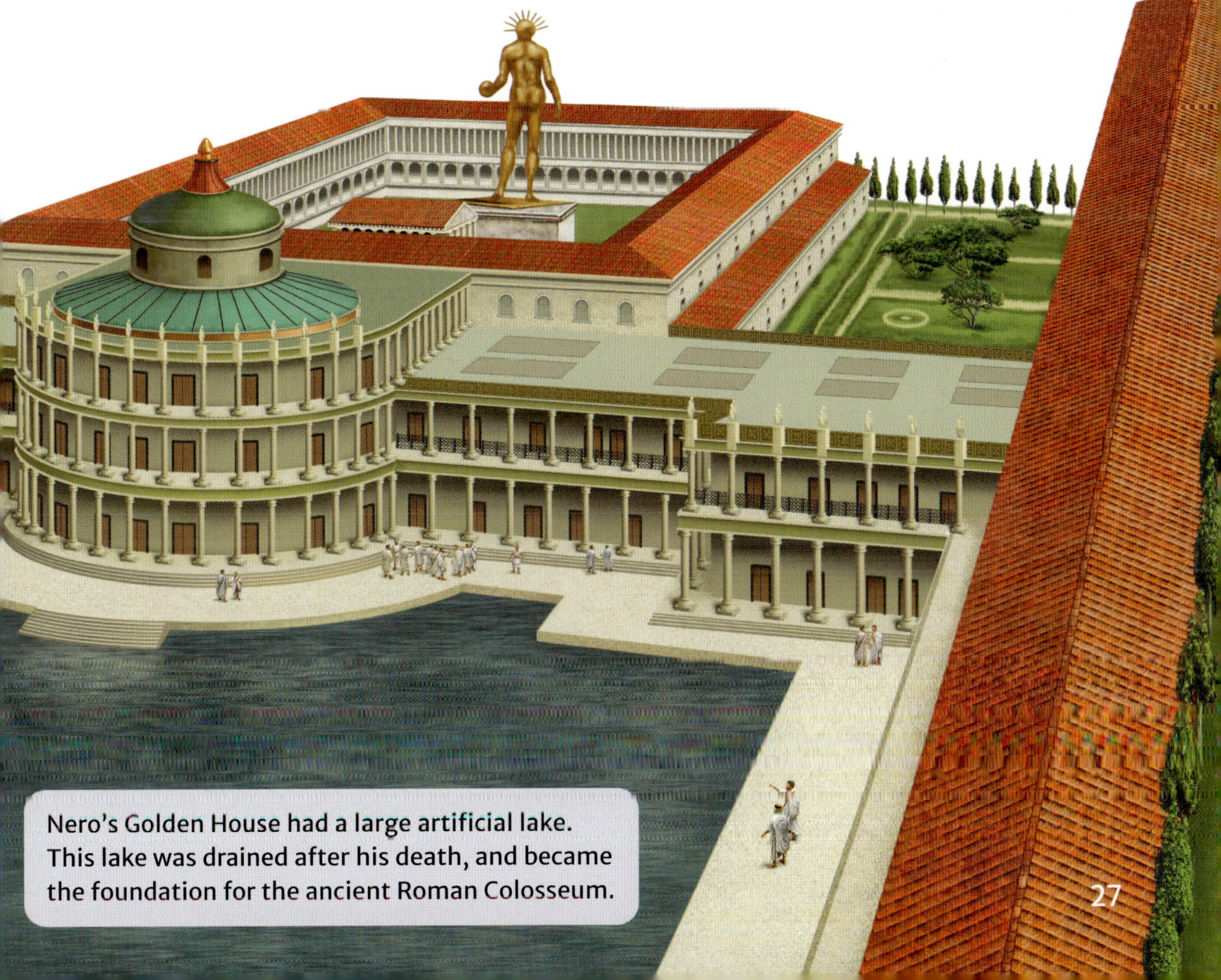

Nero's Golden House had a large artificial lake. This lake was drained after his death, and became the foundation for the ancient Roman Colosseum.

It is clear that Nero was disliked by the Roman senate, and also by the wealthier classes of Rome, to which Suetonius and Tacitus belonged. It is likely that their conscious and unconscious bias has created an inaccurate picture of Nero.

A more detailed look at the historical accounts reveals a far more complicated character than popular history depicts. Nero was passionate about the arts and enjoyed hosting and participating in typical Roman public spectacles, such as athletics and chariot racing. He sang and played the cithara (pronounced *si-ther-rah*, a type of ancient Greek lyre), and studied art, sculpture, music and poetry. These public events probably endeared him to the common people, but his artistic interests were frowned upon by the ruling classes as being unsuitable for an emperor.

While he was likely a very bad person, it is unlikely that we will ever see a clear picture of Nero.

This Roman brass coin showing Nero is a replica of one that existed during his time as emperor.

Nero enjoyed playing the cithara and performing in plays.

Fact or Fiction?

People are complex, whether they are the ruler of an empire or an enslaved person sweeping the street. Often, popular histories only tell part of the story.

Historical accounts are written for many reasons. Facts are changed and stories are made up to make a person appear heroic or evil, and the majority of people from the past have been left out of historical accounts altogether.

But what we *can* say with some certainty is that ancient historians often didn't let the truth stand in the way of a gripping story!

This statue of the Roman historian Tacitus sits outside the Austrian parliament building.

Glossary

assassination	the intentional killing of someone for political reasons
BCE	Before the Common Era; the number of years before the time dates are counted from
bribing	convincing someone to help you by giving them a gift
campaign	a series of military operations
CE	Years since the beginning of the Common Era
civil war	a war between citizens of the same country
consul	one of two elected officials who jointly ruled the Roman Republic
contemporary	living or occurring at the same time
distortions	changes to facts that make them untrue
dynasty	a line of rulers from the same family
enslaved	forced to work without pay, and not allowed to leave
Gallic	relating to the region of Gaul
omission	the act of not including information
patriotism	the quality of being devoted to one's country
privilege	rights and advantages that other people don't have

prosperity	wealth and success
Roman Empire	the empire established by Augustus Caesar in 27 BCE
Roman Republic	the ancient Roman state, which rejected monarchical power in favour of rule by the people
senate	the state council of ancient Rome
stereotypes	widely held, oversimplified ideas about a particular type of person or thing
tyrant	a cruel and oppressive ruler

Index